LEGO STAR WARS

VADER'S SECRET MISSIONS

LEGO STAR WARS®

VADER'S SECRET MISSIONS

SCHOLASTIC INC.

"The Emperor's New Clones," "Who's Afraid of the Big Bad Sith?" and "Every Darth Has His Day"
written by Ace Landers
Illustrated by Ameet Studio

LEGO, the LEGO logo, the Brick and Knob configurations and the Minifigure are trademarks of The LEGO Group. © 2015. Produced by Scholastic Inc., under license from The LEGO Group.

© 2015 Lucasfilm Ltd. ® & ™. All Rights Reserved. Used Under Authorization.

Published by Scholastic Inc., *Publishers since 1920*. SCHOLASTIC and associated logos are trademarks and/or registered trademarks of Scholastic Inc.

ISBN 978-0-545-83557-2

10 9 8 7 6 5 4 3 2   15 16 17 18 19/0
Printed in the U.S.A.   40
This edition first Scholastic printing 2015

Book design by Ameet Studio

TABLE OF CONTENTS

ON THE DARK SIDE 6

THE FALLEN JEDI 8

THE RULE OF TWO 10

THE EMPEROR'S NEW CLONES 12

THE SECRETS OF THE SITH LORDS 20

SITH LIGHTSABERS 22

EVERY DARTH HAS HIS DAY 24

THE CHOSEN ONE 40

DARTH VADER... 42

WHO'S AFRAID OF THE BIG BAD SITH?.................. 44

SITH QUIZ 60

ANSWERS 62

There is no being old enough to remember what life in the galaxy was like before the presence of the Force was first discovered. Most life-forms didn't even know about that discovery, but those who felt the mysterious energy—the so called "Force-sensitives"—knew they were experiencing something beyond their understanding.

A group of scholars, monks, and warriors from different star systems started studying the nature of the Force. Unfortunately, some of them began using their knowledge to pursue power. Soon it became clear that the energy that binds the galaxy together can be used as a dangerous weapon. Some of the users of the Force abused their abilities and became addicted to gaining more and more power. Greed, envy, and anger filled their hearts and minds. Regardless of what planet they came from, or what species they were, they had one thing in common—they followed the dark side of the Force.

There were also others, the followers of the light side of the Force—the Jedi who saw the Force as a limitless source of knowledge. For many millennia, the Jedi used their powers to keep harmony in the universe. Yet, they did not expect that one of the most powerful knights from their own ranks would turn to the dark side, help destroy the Jedi Order, and build the evil Galactic Empire. That fallen Jedi was Anakin Skywalker, later known as Darth Vader.

THE FALLEN JEDI

Anakin Skywalker was not the first, and unfortunately not the last, Jedi to renounce the Jedi values. In the old days, when the Galactic Republic was still a new formation, some Jedi chose to follow the dark side of the Force. They left the Jedi Order and used their power for personal gain. They were called the fallen Jedi.

Possessed by the lust for power, the fallen Jedi fought the Jedi Order a number of times during the next millennia. Spectacular space battles were followed by land assaults on different planets. The most serious conflict between the two factions lasted a hundred years. During the war, known as the Hundred-Year Darkness, the rogue Jedi used the dark side energies to create an army of predatory animals. The animal legions were quickly defeated, but the fallen Jedi refused to surrender. Their new monstrous creations inspired fear in the opposing armies. However, the combined forces of the Jedi Order and the Republic pushed back and ultimately defeated them.

The surviving fallen Jedi fled to the uncharted reaches of the galaxy. They landed on the world inhabited by a humanoid species calling themselves the Sith. Using their amazing ability to handle the Force, the exiled Jedi took control of the planet. The most powerful of them became the first Dark Lord of the Sith.

VADER'S CHALLENGE

The most powerful of the fallen
Jedi was called the Dull Lord of the Sith.
True or false?

THE RULE OF TWO

Cast out beyond the known space, the fallen Jedi endured. Since their arrival to Moraband, the home planet of the alien Sith race, the exiles planned to restore their power. For the next centuries, the cultures and blood mixed between the exiles and the people native to Moraband. The word *Sith* no longer referred solely to the alien race, but it generally related to the followers of the ancient Sith philosophy. The philosophy that glorified strength, conflict, and victory.

The Sith Lords still strove to destroy the Jedi and the Republic. They started conquering new territories and in the course of a thousand-year-long period of the New Sith Wars they gained control of a great part of the known galaxy, while the Republic declined. However, the battle of Ruusan ended the golden age of the New Sith Empire. The Sith were destroyed by the Jedi forces.

There was only one Sith survivor: Darth Bane. He believed that the Sith had weakened because they had accepted too many users of the Force into their ranks, and the true dark side had deserted them. Bane decided to rebuild the Sith Order as a secret organization consisting of a Sith Master and an apprentice. In this way, the dark side would fuel its great power into two beings at a time.

The Sith followed the Rule of Two and their presence remained undiscovered almost until the Clone Wars broke out. The vile schemes of Darth Sidious and his two succeeding apprentices, Darth Maul and Darth Tyranus, brought disorder in the galaxy. But when Sidious gained a new apprentice— Darth Vader—the Republic ultimately fell and the universe saw the rise of the evil Galactic Empire.

THE EMPEROR'S NEW CLONES

Even during the evil Empire's powerful reign of terror, being the Emperor wasn't easy. His generals needed constant guidance, the Rebel forces were always trying to foil his wicked plans, and he never had a moment to sit back and enjoy the fruits of his maniacal labor.

Finally, one night while he was stuck in a meeting with his top commanders, the Emperor had had enough. "It's all too much!" shouted the Emperor. "When is Vader coming back?"

"Tomorrow night, sir," answered one of the generals. "But we need to decide what to do with the Rebel prisoners, and finish the plans for the Death Star cooling system, and clean out the garbage compactors . . ."

"Stop!" demanded the Emperor. "Leave now. This meeting is over." He couldn't believe how much work he still needed to do to win this galactic war.

"I could cross off everything on my to-do list, if only there were a way that I could be in two places at one time!" And then the Emperor had a brilliant idea. He would create a clone.

The Emperor had never built a clone-making machine before, but he had seen them dozens of times. "It can't be that hard. And what's the worst that could happen?"

The Emperor sat on his throne in the Death Star, using the Force to pull brick pieces from the walls to construct a clone-making booth. The metal box sparked with energy. The clone creator was ready and the Emperor stepped inside.

"Three clones should be enough," laughed the Emperor as the doors closed around him. Blue flashes glowed brightly from inside the booth. When the doors opened, the Emperor stepped out—followed by his three clones.

"Excellent!" they all said at the same time with an evil cackle.

The next day, Darth Vader returned to the Death Star with some good news to report. However, when he walked onto the deck, he couldn't believe his nose.

"I sense a great disturbance in the . . . oh, no, what's that awful smell?!" Darth Vader gagged.

Trash covered the entire landing area, piled higher than the spaceships. "Stormtroopers! What is going on?"

"Emperor's orders, sir. We were asked to empty the garbage compactors and load the spaceships with trash."

"That's the worst idea I've ever heard!" said Darth Vader. He jumped as several tentacled creatures popped their eyestalks up through the smelly waste. "Put it all back in the compactors immediately—including those slimy dianogas! Where's the Emperor?"

"He's up with the prisoners," answered another storm-trooper.

Vader hurried up to the prison level, but when he arrived the cells were empty and the Emperor was sweeping the floors!

"Master! What are you doing cleaning this place?" asked Darth Vader. "And where are the Rebel prisoners?"

"Oh, I let them go," the Emperor admitted. "They were so nice and their rooms were filthy, so I decided to give the place a good scrub."

"You did what?!" screamed Vader. "I'm sorry, Master, but . . . wait a minute, why are you cleaning with your hands? You should be using the Force." And then Vader realized what was going on. "You're a clone—and not a very good one!"

Vader Force Pushed the clone back into a cell and set off to undo the damage. He made an announcement over the

sound system. "Attention, guards, be on the lookout for Rebel prisoners. The Emperor has . . . um . . . sent them down to help clean up the mess on the landing deck. But they should be recaptured immediately."

Then Vader turned and felt another disturbance in the Force. It was coming from the Emperor's quarters.

When he arrived, Vader found another Emperor clone typing into a computer. "What are you doing?" Vader asked.

"I've finally figured out how to make the Death Star airtight!" the clone cheered. "If we just close up this small thermal exhaust port, the station will be indestructible!"

"No, no, no!" said Vader. "One clone freed all the captives and one clone spread trash everywhere. I don't need your faulty notes making our greatest weapon implode because the core overheats! Now, where's the real Emperor?!"

But then a blast rang out through the room! It was the Rebel prisoners! Vader was knocked into an odd-looking metal booth in the room, but the Emperor clone wasn't as lucky. The Rebels captured him, cheering as they took him away.

As Vader stood up, the metal booth began to hum and glow. It stopped as suddenly as it had begun. "*Hrmph*." Vader shrugged. "That was weird."

Vader poked his head out of the booth and heard a very quiet noise coming from behind the Emperor's throne. He turned the large chair around to discover the real Emperor

playing video games with his headphones on.

"Vader!" he screamed. "I was going to break my high score but you made me crash!"

"But, Master," Vader said, "your clones are destroying your evil Empire!"

The Emperor gulped. "I just wanted some 'me' time!"

"You built a clone-maker?" said Vader. "That's a terrible idea! If not properly made, clones come out broken and can make a real mess of things."

"Then, I guess you better go take care of my clones while I finish this level," the Emperor laughed, putting his headphones back on.

Vader turned to see his three clones destroying the room. Vader ignited his lightsaber. "I always get the hard jobs."

THE SECRETS
OF THE SITH LORDS

The Jedi fought the Sith Lords for many millennia, but they never managed to discover all of their greatest enemy's secrets. Here are some interesting facts about the Sith Lords.

The title of Dark Lord of the Sith originally referred to the ruler of the Sith Empire. Later it was given to the recognized leader of the Order of the Sith Lords. The first to use that title was Ajunta Pall, the leader of the exiled Dark Jedi who conquered the Sith species on Moraband.

The reigning Dark Lord of the Sith had a group of advisors who formed the Sith Council within the Sith Empire. The Council consisted of ten Sith Lords who managed the affairs of the Empire. Each Lord that sat on the Council ruled over at least twelve worlds.

Under the command of Lord Kaan, the Sith amassed a great number of powerful battleships unique to their fleet. Their crews were driven by Kaan's battle meditation (a Force ability that boosted their combat prowess), whereby Kaan and his followers used their dark powers to create destructive "thought bombs."

The Sith Lords were known to have practiced Force alchemy. They used primarily dark-side energies to enhance the strength of weapons and armor, but they also experimented by creating life-forms, like the monstrous creatures used in many battles. Darth Sidious was a true master of this dark art.

After death, the Sith Lords were buried in the Valley of the Dark Lords on Moraband. The tombtown was protected by Moraband Sith zombies—undead humanoid predators created with the use of ancient Sith alchemy and magic. The creatures could also create more of their kind by biting living beings.

The Sith often had scary tattoos. The application of the complicated patterns on the entire body was very painful, because it was done by Sith pincerbugs. The bugs' burning venom was also used during the initiation of a new Dark Lord of the Sith to burn the Dark Lord's mark on his forehead.

VADER'S CHALLENGE

The burial site of the Sith Lords was called the Valley of the Sith Zombies.
True or false?

SITH LIGHTSABERS

When the dark-siders rebelled against the Jedi Order, they used protosabers—the original Jedi weapon—to fight their former brothers. At the end of the conflict, the defeated dark Jedi were disarmed and exiled beyond the Republic territory. But when they landed on Moraband, it turned out that quite a few of them had managed to keep their weapons.

The ancient Sith traditionally wielded forged swords with metal blades. Some of the exiles who made themselves the new Sith Lords preferred to use a sword instead of a protosaber. Enhanced with the Sith alchemy, the swords focused the dark energy of their wielders, amplifying their power and refining their control of the Force.

Nevertheless, inspired by the Jedi weapons, the Sith quickly developed their weaponry. The protosaber evolved into an early version of a much more effective and powerful lightsaber. A miniaturized power cell inside the hilt enabled the emission of a focused energy blade capable of cutting through almost any substance or deflecting blaster bolts. The typical red glow of the Sith single-bladed or double-bladed lightsabers resulted from the use of synthetic focusing crystals infused with the dark energies. In time, the red blades became the symbol of the fierce power and terror of the Sith Lords.

VADER'S CHALLENGE

Sith lightsabers can deflect blaster bolts.
True or false?

EVERY DARTH HAS HIS DAY

A s Darth Vader and his squad of three TIE fighters sped through hyperspace, he knew one thing for certain: They were very, very lost.

"Where in the galaxy are we?" he asked one of the TIE fighter pilots in his unit.

"Sir?" said the pilot nervously as he unraveled a large space map. "According to my calculations, we should be near the training zone now . . . hopefully."

Vader had planned to meet the Black Squadron in the Outer Rim Territories to practice some attack maneuvers. But even through the elongated stars of hyperspace, Vader sensed they were off course. "I find your lack of direction disturbing," growled Vader. "We're going to be late. Disengage hyperdrive."

"Of course, Lord Vader," said the pilot.

Slowly, the blurred white lines came into focus, becoming stars and something else unexpected . . . a Rebel X-wing. Vader quickly veered to avoid the X-wing's attack, but the other TIE fighter pilots weren't as prepared. "Ha, you missed!" Vader laughed. But then a stray blast hit one of the wings on his TIE Advanced x1.

"Now I'm going to be really late," Vader huffed as his TIE fighter flipped through space out of control. "What is an X-wing doing all the way out here by itself, anyway?" Just as Vader was regaining control of his ship, he found himself stuck in the gravitational pull of the nearest planet.

Bracing for impact, the Sith Lord rattled in his TIE fighter as it skipped violently across the frozen tundra until coming to a rest against a snowy mountain. Vader pulled himself from the hatch and felt the frigid wind whip around him. There was nothing but snow for as far as he could see.

"Hoth," said Vader with a chill in his voice. "Why did it have to be Hoth?"

The ice planet wasn't anywhere near where they were going to meet the Black Squadron for training. He also knew that one X-wing meant that there must be more nearby, and the Rebels would be looking for him soon enough. Unfortunately, his dark suit stood out against the white snow like a droid in the Mos Eisley cantina. He needed to find a hiding place as fast as possible.

The ship's communicator was ruined, so Vader couldn't call for help. "This must be my lucky day," he moaned. Setting off a tracking beacon, he hoped that the Black Squadron might pick up the signal and come rescue him. But staying here waiting wasn't safe, so he walked away from the wreckage. He hadn't traveled far before discovering a set of tauntaun tracks that led to a giant boulder lodged against the foot of a mountain.

With a Force Push, Vader swept the rock aside to reveal a hidden ice cave.

"Hello . . . ?" said Vader into the darkness. "Anyone—or anything—home?" But there was no answer, so he continued into the cave. He was glad to be under cover and out of the cold, and was just about to rub his sore feet when he heard something.

Voices! It was a pair of Rebel soldiers walking by and talking loudly.

"Whew, you think this place is cold now, wait until nightfall!

It drops down to minus sixty degrees!" said one soldier who walked with a swagger.

"Totally, Han. This is the perfect place for our Rebel prison!" said Luke. "If these criminals try to escape, they'll freeze their tauntauns off!"

"That's if they get past the wampas first," said Han with a chuckle.

"Good one!" replied Luke. "But seriously, wampas can't get us in here—right?"

"No way, kid," said Han. "This secret cave is airtight! Now, let's get back and check on the prisoners."

Vader hid in the darkness and watched as the Rebels walked through a metal door that slid open and shut behind them.

"So, it seems I've stumbled onto a Rebel base," laughed Vader. "With prisoners, no less. But the Empire isn't missing any members. Who do those Rebels have trapped here?"

There was only one way to find out. Vader snuck through the shadows and followed the Rebels inside.

Beyond the metal door was a sparsely built hangar filled with spaceships. As Vader wandered through the tarmac, Rebel pilots were gearing up for a search mission.

"I swear, it had to be Vader that we shot down," said one soldier. "Who else would have a TIE Advanced x1 with the words THE DARTHNESS painted on the side?"

"Well, if he's on Hoth, you bet we'll find him," said another soldier.

Vader switched directions to avoid contact. He needed to find the prison because whoever was locked up here may be his only hope of escaping. Using a Rebel computer, Vader located the prison. He was about to go inside when he heard a familiar voice behind him.

"Aren't you a little short for Darth Vader?" asked Luke.

Vader wheeled around and held his mechanical breath. It took every ounce of Force inside him to not attack this mini-Rebel right then and there. There was something oddly familiar about this kid.

"I'm just kidding, buddy," laughed Luke. "Listen, soldier, I don't know where you got that costume, but you should take it off in case people think you're the *real* Vader and they, you know, attack you."

As Luke walked away laughing, he added, "On second thought, keep the costume on and go give the prisoners a good scare!"

Vader gave Luke a nod in agreement and entered the prison. There behind the jail cell bars sat almost every ruthless

bounty hunter Darth Vader knew: Boba Fett, Bossk, Zuckuss, IG-88, and even that hideous Dengar were pacing back and forth like animals trapped in cages.

"It's Darth Vader!" screamed one of the Rebel guards. But before the guard could sound the alarm, Vader used the Force to construct a jail cell around them out of bricks.

"Whoa!" said Dengar in amazement. "Darth Vader to the rescue! Now I've seen everything."

"Come on!" commanded Vader as he ignited his lightsaber. "Follow me to freedom." The Sith Lord sliced the control board in half and the jail cells opened. Stealthily, the bounty hunters exited and gathered their weapons.

"Can I blow up the Rebel base?" asked Boba Fett.

"No, no, no!" ordered Vader. "We need to get out of here unnoticed. Then I can bring back the entire Imperial fleet and crush the Rebels once and for—"

An explosion rocked the entire base. "Whoops," said the assassin droid IG-88, who had accidentally set off a concussion grenade he picked up with his weapons. Half of the prison wall was gone and the stunned faces of the Rebel fighters stared back at them.

"You programmable fool!" cried Vader. "All of you, follow me!"

Vader launched directly into the Rebels, Force Pushing them aside. The bounty hunters took his lead and attacked. It was madness and mayhem in the Rebels' not-so-secret base.

Instantly, another flood of Rebel soldiers stormed in, but Vader arranged bricks to build a staircase that led over the Rebel crew. Bossk, Zuckuss, and Dengar ran up the stairs after him.

"What's the plan now?" asked Dengar.

"We head over to that fleet of X-wings that are prepared to launch," called out Vader as he raced for the ships. "Then we

blast off and leave these Rebels in our dark-side dust."

But before Vader could reach the ships, those Rebel heroes, Luke and Han, bravely blocked his path.

"The real Darth Vader!" said Luke. "Well, well, well. Now it looks like we've got you sur—" But before Luke could finish his sentence a wampa rushed in and grabbed him!

Han chased after the wampa to save Luke. "I hate to say it, kid, but I was wrong about the wampas!"

Suddenly, the coast was clear and Darth Vader motioned for the bounty hunters to board the X-wings.

"Ah, finally," said Vader as he and the fleet of bounty hunters started their engines and flew into the safety of space. Vader used the communicator to send out a message: "Emperor, this is Darth Vader. We have found a hidden Rebel base on Hoth."

"Excellent, Vader," came the Emperor's swift reply. "We've just arrived nearby and we see their X-wings in our sights now."

"You do?" Vader asked, looking around. He could see the Black Squadron, and their guns were aimed at him. Then he realized—the Emperor didn't know he and the other bad guys were in the X-wings. "Wait, don't fire!" Vader shouted into the communicator. But it was too late. The X-wings exploded.

"This was a terrible rescue!" Boba Fett shouted at Vader as they floated among the space debris.

"Worst day ever," Vader whined as he drifted aimlessly in outer space. "Any idea how we can get home now?"

THE CHOSEN ONE

If there was one thing that made some beings more sensitive to the Force than others, it was their midi-chlorian count. Midi-chlorians were intelligent microscopic life-forms living in the cells of all living things across the galaxy. A being's potential in using the Force depended on a high midi-chlorian count in their blood.

The reports that a being with the highest known midi-chlorian count was found thrilled the Jedi. It was a young human named Anakin Skywalker. When the boy was brought to the Jedi Council meeting, some Jedi believed he was the prophesized "Chosen One" who would bring balance to the Force. Others were very hesitant about Anakin's potential to become a true Jedi. They saw too much fear and anger in him.

Despite the advice from the Council, Qui-Gon Jinn—the Jedi who had found Anakin—took the boy as an apprentice. After Qui-Gon's sudden death, Obi-Wan Kenobi continued to instruct Anakin. Over the years, Skywalker turned from a boy into a young, but very powerful, Jedi. Yet, his defiant nature often made him question the ways of the Jedi or defy his superiors and friends.

Soon the darkness reached out for Anakin. Darth Sidious, acting in disguise as the respected Chancellor Palpatine, saw an opportunity to acquire a new, promising apprentice. Sidious cunningly incited anger and hatred in the heart of the troubled Jedi and finally turned him to the dark side. The Jedi's "Chosen One" became the Lord of the Sith known as Darth Vader.

Sidious and Vader, the Sith Master and his apprentice, destroyed the Jedi and led to the fall of the Galactic Republic. The rule of the Galactic Empire began.

DARTH VADER

The clash between Vader and his former Master, Obi-Wan Kenobi, was inevitable. But a fierce duel on Mustafar ended badly for the young Sith. Vader was defeated and suffered nearly lethal injuries.

At the Emperor's orders, Vader's body was almost entirely reconstructed. His severed limbs were replaced with cybernetic ones—the updated version of the same technology that had transformed General Grievous into a cyborg. In addition, Vader had to wear a protective suit for the rest of his life.

Filled with multiple life-support systems, the suit encased Vader completely. It was constructed using secret methods of Sith alchemy that amplified Vader's diminished strength and vitality. However, in the early years, the suit limited his vision, restrained his movement, and caused extreme frustration.

In order to make up for the lack of mobility caused by the suit, Vader changed his fighting style. He longed to be less dependent on his suit, even though it was upgraded, but he couldn't function without it. He removed it only for a short time inside his meditation chamber, a hyperbaric sphere that was super-oxygenated.

Vader's robotic limbs and all of the armor's functions were powered by multiple energy cells located throughout the suit. Vader was always equipped with emergency backup cells to replace the depleted ones, but usually he would recharge his suit within one of his spherical meditation chambers.

Formed after the ancient Sith droids, Vader's black suit was also a durable and fireproof piece of armor. His gloves were made with a unique micronized iron that could even deflect blaster bolts. Thanks to an internal oxygen supply, the mask and armor could also serve as an airtight spacesuit for a short time.

Though Vader was still very powerful, his injuries had robbed him of much of his Force potential. In addition, he suspected that the Emperor deliberately ordered not to use the most advanced technology for the reconstruction of his body, because he didn't want Vader to be strong enough to rebel against him.

VADER'S CHALLENGE

Encased within the armored suit, Vader's partly cybernetic body did not need nourishment. True or false?

WHO'S AFRAID OF THE BIG BAD SITH?

Hidden in the vast forests of Kashyyyk, Darth Vader, the evil Sith Lord, nodded in approval. "Excellent, the Disconnector is fully operational," he said between slow, clicking breaths.

Next to Vader, the Emperor sneezed. "You had better not waste my time on this flea-ridden planet, Vader. I'm allergic to Wookiees! So, how does your new contraption work?"

The weapon looked like a mix between a giant cannon and an oversized flashlight. The chamber sizzled and crackled with energy as it cooled down after its first test run.

"Oh, I think you'll be pleased, Master. By pulling apart all of the bricks, the Disconnector makes building any technology

out of bricks impossible," said Vader proudly. "Spaceships, secret bases, cities, nothing will be safe from the Empire anymore."

"*Hmmm,*" said the Emperor. "I still like my Death Star idea."

"It blew up, Master, remember?" said Vader.

"Which is precisely why I think we should build a new one," said the Emperor.

Vader let out a huge sigh. "We've been over this, Master. Why would we ever build the same thing twice? The Rebels would just blow up the Death Star again if they had the chance."

"You don't know that," argued the Emperor.

"Master," huffed Vader. "You've known me for a long time

now. I'm a destroyer, not a builder. Besides, we tried your idea already. Now it's time to try mine."

"All right, all right. Then show me," said the Emperor.

"First, you'll need these," said Vader, handing the Emperor a pair of sunglasses as a stormtrooper wheeled out a giant video screen that showed an Imperial Star Destroyer in outer space.

"That's one of our spaceships," said the Emperor.

"It was," said Darth Vader as he engaged the Disconnector.

A blast erupted from Darth's new weapon, sending a blinding beam of light into the sky. On the screen, the Imperial Star Destroyer was suddenly surrounded by the brightness. Instantly, the giant ship halted in the light's grip and began to slide apart, brick by brick, until it had been completely dismantled. A moment after the otherworldly blast began, it ceased, leaving only the floating flotsam and jetsam of tiny pieces that once made up the massive spaceship.

The Emperor pulled off his sunglasses. "Vader, you're a genius."

"Thank you, Master," said Vader.

"And you're an idiot, too," snapped the Emperor. "That Star Destroyer was our ride home!"

"I, uh, um," stuttered Darth Vader nervously, "well, at least we know the Disconnector works. Besides, I've never been terribly fond of Star Destroyers. They've always looked like giant tortilla chips to me."

"What I want to know is why you didn't test the Disconnector on a Rebel spaceship?" asked the Emperor.

"Where am I going to find a Rebel ship around here, Master?" asked Vader.

"How about that one?" the Emperor said, pointing to the video screen. Among the wreckage floating in space, the *Millennium Falcon* zipped into view.

"Looks like it's my lucky day," laughed Vader as he took aim at the Rebel ship.

"Just fire at them before they get *a-a-a*—!" sniffled the Emperor until he let out a giant sneeze. *"ACHOO!"* Instantly a bolt of Sith lightning exploded forth from the Emperor, accidentally zapping the team and the Disconnector.

"Stupid Wookiee planet!" wheezed the Emperor.

Frizzled but focused, Darth Vader quickly shook off the shock and fired the Disconnector, but the blast missed its mark. Instead of blasting the *Millennium Falcon* with a direct hit, it struck and dismantled the ship's rear engines.

Vader and the Emperor watched as the *Millennium Falcon*

fell from space and burst through the cloud cover. The spaceship was damaged, but still flying. It swooped down with a rain of blasts aimed at Vader and his newest weapon.

The Sith Lord quickly tried to fire the Disconnector again, but the trigger fell off thanks to another of the Emperor's surprise sneeze attacks. Laser blasts landed all around Vader, but he stood his ground.

Without its engines, the *Millennium Falcon* cruised over Vader and brushed against the treetops until it crash-landed in the distant woods.

"Well, that could have gone better," said the Emperor as he climbed out from his hiding place behind a tree.

Vader turned in the direction of the wrecked ship, ignited his lightsaber, then climbed on a speeder bike. "I want those Rebels . . . dead or alive!"

On board the *Millennium Falcon*, Han fought the controls as Chewie looked for a safe place to land. In the distance there was a small break in the forest where a river ran peacefully.

"Brace yourself, everyone!" yelled Han as the ship scraped against the treetops. Finally, the forest ended, and Han cruised into the riverbed and found a dry place to touch down.

"Guys, I promise," pleaded Luke Skywalker. "I had a strong hunch about that Imperial Star Destroyer. I mean, one Star Destroyer by itself near Kashyyyk? It doesn't make sense."

"Yes, it does," said Princess Leia as she unlatched herself from a safety harness. "It was a trap."

"It wasn't a trap," snapped Luke.

"Trust us, kid. It's always a trap," said Han. "Now, let's get out and see what's wrong with this ship before tall, dark, and evil shows up."

Luke was the first off the ship followed by Han, Leia, and Chewie. The entire backside of the *Millennium Falcon* had come completely undone.

"AAARRGGHHHH!" cried Chewie.

"I agree," said Han, surveying the damage. "Whatever did this is dangerous. We were lucky."

Just then the hum of Imperial speeders echoed through the forest. "Looks like we've got visitors," said Luke as he swiftly ran into the woods.

The scout troopers whisked through the forest and finally found the *Millennium Falcon*. Vader stepped off his speeder as the Imperial team boarded the ship to search for the Rebels.

"They're not on the ship, you fools," commanded Vader. "They're hiding in the trees!"

Luke leaped first, knocking a trooper off his speeder bike. Then Han and Leia used a vine to clothesline two more troopers to the ground, while Chewie simply snagged the last trooper and threw him against a tree. The Rebels leaped onto the speeder bikes and took off.

"Ugh, do I have to do everything myself?" Vader complained as he jumped back on his speeder and chased after the Rebels.

Whipping through the trees, Han shouted at Luke, "Do you even know where you're going?"

"I've got another one of those feelings," said Luke. "We've got to find Vader's new weapon and destroy it."

But before Han could answer, Vader Force Pushed him off his speeder, sending him tumbling head over heels into a bush. His speeder slammed into a tree and exploded into pieces.

"You're next, Skywalker!" hollered Vader as he surged forward. He wielded his lightsaber and held it aloft, ready to crash it down on Luke—but Leia and Chewie surrounded him.

Vader thrashed at the two Rebels, but the Wookiee caught his arm and wrestled the lightsaber out of his grip. It landed with a thud in the dirt. Vader struggled against the Wookiee's powerful clutches while kicking Leia away. Her speeder flew off in another direction, narrowly missing tree trunks along the way. Then the Sith Lord finally freed one hand and called forth his lost lightsaber, which flew through the forest and into his hand. He ignited the lightsaber and slashed through Chewie's speeder, sending the big ball of fuzz careening to the forest floor.

With Luke still in the lead, Vader left the other Rebels behind and raced back to the Emperor before the young Jedi could get there first.

Back at the Disconnector, the Emperor was trying to fix their new weapon. *"Hmmm,"* said the Emperor. "How long does it take to capture Rebels in a crashed ship? Vader should have been back by now."

Almost on cue, Vader arrived and flipped off of his bike. "Am I too late?"

"Too late for what?" asked the Emperor as the hum of other speeder bikes echoed through the forest. "Ah, sounds like our scout troopers are just around the corner with those Rebels," said the Emperor, but when he turned around, two unmanned speeder bikes dashed out of the darkness heading straight for them.

Quickly, Darth Vader shoved the bikes aside with a Force Push, but a third bike flew in from a different direction. The Emperor unleashed a Force lightning blast that scorched the bike, exploding it into a cloud of smoke and debris before it could strike its intended target.

"What kind of awful driving do they teach in scout trooper school?!" hollered the Emperor.

"Master," said Darth Vader, "this wasn't the work of poorly trained scout troopers."

"He's right, Your Evilness," said Luke Skywalker as he stepped out from behind a tree. "Now, give up. We've got you surrounded."

"Hardly," laughed the Emperor as his rotting teeth gleamed under the shade of the swaying treetops. With a swipe of his hand,

Han, Leia, and Chewie were all dragged into the opening against their will. "Only four puny Rebels? And you—*a-a-a-ACHOO!*"

"Okay, seriously, Master, what is up with all this sneezing?" asked Darth Vader.

"It's Wookiee hair," said the Emperor. "Nothing to worry about, I'm sure. Now, where was I? Oh, yes. Poor young Skywalker, you truly didn't think your heroic attack through, now did you?"

"Honestly, I did not," said Luke with a frown. The remaining scout troopers took his friends into custody, while Darth Vader and the Emperor laughed.

"I hate to crush your spirit and run, Skywalker," said Darth Vader as Emperor Palpatine's shuttle finally arrived. "But there's still a secret Rebel base to find. Once we build a new Disconnector with these secret plans, we will blast it to bric-a-brac smithereens and it will be bye-bye, Rebels—hello, total domination!"

Luke glared at Vader holding up the secret plans, but then he saw something reflected in the Sith Lord's dark mask. A furry shape moved quietly behind the trees. In fact, there was a lot of moving going on behind the trees all around them, but Vader and the Emperor were too busy laughing to notice. The hair, the Emperor's sneezing fits . . . It all suddenly made sense.

"You'll never get away with this," said Luke. "I'm going to stop you."

"You and whose army?" asked Vader.

"Me and that army," said Luke as ten Wookiees stepped out from the forest. Towering over the scout troopers, the tall and furry warriors growled. The remaining stormtroopers took a few steps back.

"Ha!" laughed Vader. "We can fry up ten Wookiees in no time—right, Master?"

But the Emperor looked very worried. "Vader . . . *ACHOO!* we're not—*ACHOO!*—dealing with—*ACHOO!*—just ten—*ACHOO!*—Wookiees."

Instantly, a hundred Wookiees made their presence known by calling into the sky. Chewbacca also joined their growling chant.

"Impossible!" cried Vader. "I thought we had Kashyyyk under our control."

"Well," said the Emperor, "not all of Kashyyyk apparently."

"Now, the way I see things, you little Sithies," Han said with a smirk, "is that you have one choice: give up!"

"Not my style," said Darth Vader as he and the Emperor

leaped high into the air, where the Emperor's shuttle was waiting for them.

But Luke used the Force to nab the secret plans for the Disconnector right out of Vader's grip. *"Noooooo!!!!"* Vader screamed.

The Sith Lord lunged to attack the Rebels and the Wookiee army, but the Emperor grabbed his cape and tugged him onto the spaceship.

"Not now, Vader! *ACHOO!*" cried the Emperor. "I'm having— *ACHOO!*—a major—*ACHOO!*—Wookiee allergy attack! *ACHOO!* The farther we are from this planet, the better. Now, let's go build that second Death Star already, and I promise . . . We'll be back!"

So the Sith Lords flew off into space and escaped, but their secret weapon was now in Rebel hands.

SITH QUIZ

The eternal conflict between the powers of good and evil will continue. Meanwhile, check what you have learned from this book. Read the questions and mark the correct answer to each of them.

1. What was so special about the Force-sensitive beings?
   a) They didn't have a sense of humor.
   b) They could feel and use the Force.
   c) They fed on the dark side of the Force.

2. What planet did the exiled fallen Jedi land on?
   a) Moraband
   b) Ruusan
   c) Umbara

3. Who introduced the Rule of Two?
   a) Darth Sidious
   b) Darth Bane
   c) Darth Vader

4. How were the Sith tattoos traditionally applied?
   a) By hand, with an erasable pen
   b) By spray paint
   c) By venomous bugs

5. How many worlds did a member of the Sith Council rule?
   a) None
   b) One
   c) Twelve

6. What was the color of the Sith lightsaber blades?
   a) Red
   b) Green
   c) Black

7. What was so special about Vader's gloves?
   a) They used to belong to General Grievous.
   b) The left one was a bit too tight.
   c) They could deflect blaster shots.

8. Who was not an apprentice of Darth Sidious?
   a) Darth Maul
   b) Darth Bane
   c) Darth Tyranus

9. What did the prophecy say about the "Chosen One"?
   a) He would restore the power of the Sith in the galaxy.
   b) He would bring balance to the Force.
   c) He would destroy the Jedi and the Republic.

10. What was the name of the "Chosen One"?
    a) Obi-Wan Kenobi
    b) Qui-Gon Jinn
    c) Anakin Skywalker

ANSWERS

Page 9
The Fallen Jedi
False. At the beginning, the ones who turned to the dark side were called the fallen Jedi. Ever since the fallen Jedi settled on Moraband and became the Sith, the most powerful ones were granted the title of Dark Lord of the Sith.

Page 21
The Secrets of the Sith Lords
False. It was called the Valley of the Dark Lords and it was originally known as the Valley of the Sleeping Kings.

Page 23
Sith Lightsabers
True. Sith lightsabers can deflect blaster bolts as well as cut through almost anything.

Page 43
Darth Vader
False. After the reconstruction, Vader still needed food just like any other living being. Even with the mask covering his face, Vader could still eat, but only when he was inside his meditation chamber, since he had to open his triangular respiratory vent in order to take food. He preferred liquids, but he could still chew, if he wished.

Pages 60-61
Sith Quiz
1 – b, 2 – a, 3 – b, 4 – c, 5 – c, 6 – a, 7 – c, 8 – b, 9 – b, 10 – c.

DISCOVER MORE LEGO® STAR WARS™ BOOKS!

Evil powers are scheming to take control of the peaceful Galactic Republic! But as long as the brave Jedi led by Master Yoda are on the watch, the galaxy is safe . . .

Read about the adventures of Jedi Master Yoda in these other LEGO® *Star Wars*™ books: